WHERE IS ROBIN?

By Maggie Testa

Illustrated by Patrick Spaziante

Batman created by Bob Kane with Bill Finger

Ready-to-Read

Simon Spotlight

New York   London   Toronto   Sydney   New Delhi

Here is a list of all the words you will find in this book.
Sound them out before you begin reading the story.

Names:

Batman

The Joker

Robin

SIMON SPOTLIGHT
An imprint of Simon & Schuster Children's Publishing Division
1230 Avenue of the Americas, New York, New York 10020 · This Simon Spotlight edition August 2018
All rights reserved, including the right of reproduction in whole or in part in any form.
SIMON SPOTLIGHT, READY-TO-READ, and colophon are registered trademarks of Simon & Schuster, Inc.
For information about special discounts for bulk purchases, please contact Simon & Schuster Special Sales at
1-866-506-1949 or business@simonandschuster.com. Manufactured in the United States of America 0718 LAK
2 4 6 8 10 9 7 5 3 1 · ISBN 978-1-5344-2596-5 (hc) · ISBN 978-1-5344-2595-8 (pbk) · ISBN 978-1-5344-2597-2 (eBook)

Word families:

long "-e" ⟶ be   he   see

long "-o" ⟶ go   no

Sight words:

and	are	can	find
here	is	not	there
where	will	yes	

Bonus word:

| cannot | | |

Ready to go? Happy reading!

Don't miss the questions about the story
on the last page of this book.

Where is Robin?

Batman will find
Robin.

Batman will go here.

Is Robin here?

No.

Batman will go there.

Is Robin there?

No.

Robin is not here.

The Joker is here.

Is Robin here?

No.

The Joker is there.

Is Robin there?

Yes!

The Joker cannot see
Batman.

Robin can see
Batman.

Batman and Robin are here.

The Joker is there.

Now that you have read the story, can you answer these questions?

1. Where did Batman find Robin?

2. Why could Robin see Batman, but the Joker could not?

3. In this story, you read the words "yes" and "no." Those words are opposites. Can you think of other words that are opposites?

Great job!
You are a reading star!